IRISH
Legends
for children

Retold by
Yvonne Carroll

Illustrated by
Lucy Su

DERRYDALE BOOKS
New York • Avenel

Contents

Introduction

These much-loved Irish legends
have been passed down from
generation to generation.

The exciting adventures of the
Red Branch Knights and the
Fianna are retold here. They tell
of incredible acts of heroism and
mysterious magical happenings,
many of them symbolizing the
journey from childhood to
adulthood. Read about the
Children of Lir becoming
beautiful, white swans; how
Fionn defeats the fire-breathing
dragon; and whether or not
Oisín returns from Tír na n-Óg,
the land of eternal youth.

The beauty and mystery of the
tales are enhanced by charming
illustrations throughout.

Children of Lir

Once upon a time there lived a king called Lir who had four children: a daughter named Fionnuala and three sons called Aodh, Fiachra and Con.

Their mother the queen was dead, and the children were sad because they missed her terribly. They missed the stories she used to tell them, the games she used to play, and the songs she sang at bedtime as she hugged them to sleep.

The king saw that his children were sad and needed a mother, so he decided to marry again. His new bride was called Aoife. She was beautiful, but she was not the kindhearted person the king thought she was.

Aoife grew jealous of the four children because their father loved them so much. She wanted the king all to herself, so she planned to get rid of the children. She asked a druid to help her, and together they thought up a terrible spell.

5

In the castle grounds there was a lovely lake which the children spent most of their time playing beside. One day Aoife went with the children to the lakeside. As they played in the water, she suddenly pulled out a magic wand and waved it over them. There was a flash of light, and the children vanished. In their place were four beautiful white swans.

One of the swans opened its beak and spoke with Fionnuala's voice: "Oh, what have you done to us?" she asked, in a frightened voice.

"I have put a
spell on you,"
replied Aoife. "Now everything
you have will be mine. You
will be swans for nine hundred
years. You will spend three
hundred years on this lake,
three hundred years on the Sea
of Moyle and three hundred
years on the Isle of Glora.
Only the sound of a church
bell can break
the spell."

When the children did not
come home that evening, the
king went to look for them by
the lake. As he came near,
four swans swam up to him.
He was amazed when they
began to call out.
"Father, father," they cried,
"we are your children. Aoife
has placed a terrible magic
spell on us."

The king ran back to the castle and pleaded with Aoife to change the swans back into children, but she refused. Now he saw how selfish she was and banished her from the kingdom. Lir promised a reward to anyone who could break the spell, but nobody knew how.

Lir spent the rest of his life beside the lake, talking to his children, until he grew old and died. The swans were heartbroken. They no longer talked or sang, and nobody came to see them.

Three hundred years passed
and it was time for the swans
to move to the cold and stormy
Sea of Moyle between Ireland
and Scotland.

The poor swans
were tossed
about by the
wild waves

and dashed against sharp
rocks. It was a harsh life
with little food and the
years passed slowly.

When the time came for them
to fly to the Isle of Glora, the
swans were old and tired.
Although it was warmer on
the island and there was
lots of food, they were still
very lonely.

Then one day they
heard the sound
they had waited
nine hundred years
for. It was the sound
of a church bell.

The bell was ringing in the tower of a little church. An old man, called Caomhóg, stood outside. He was amazed to hear swans talking and listened to their sad story in astonishment. Then he went inside his church and brought out some holy water which he sprinkled on the swans while he prayed. As soon as the water touched them, the swans miraculously began to change into an old, old woman and three old, old men.

Lir's children were frightened.
Caomhóg told them about
God and his love for all
people. They no longer felt
scared. Fionnuala put her arms
around her brothers and all
four old people fell to the
ground, dead.

Caomhóg buried them in one
grave. That night he dreamed
he saw four swans flying up
through the clouds and he
knew that the children of Lir
were at last on their way
to Heaven to be with
their mother and
father again.

Deirdre of the Sorrows

When the baby Deirdre was born, her father, Feidhlim, asked the wise druids to look at the stars and tell him what the future held for her.

The wise druids answered: "This baby will cause great trouble. She will grow up to be the most beautiful woman in Ulster, but she will cause the death of many of our men."

When the Red Branch Knights of
Ulster heard this they were very
worried for their lives. They went
to King Connor demanding that
baby Deirdre be killed.

The king thought for a while.
"I have the answer," he said.
"Deirdre will be brought up far
away from here and when she is
old enough I will marry her."

Deirdre was taken away at once to a deep wood. The king chose a wise old woman, called Leabharcham, to care for her and teach her. As Deirdre grew older she became as beautiful as the druids had foretold. She had long golden hair and deep blue eyes. However, she was a very lonely girl.

One day, Deirdre told
Leabharcham about a dream she
had every night.
"I dream of a tall dark warrior.
His hair is as black as the
raven. His skin is as white
as snow. He is
fearless in battle."
Leabharcham was
worried as she knew
the man Deirdre
dreamed about.
"He is Naoise, one
of the Sons of
Uisneach.
You must never
mention your dream
again. You will be
married to King
Connor very soon,"
she said.

17

Deirdre begged Leabharcham to
send for Naoise so she might meet
the man of her dreams.

At first Leabharcham refused but
she hated to see Deirdre unhappy
and she gave in. Deirdre and
Naoise met and they fell in love
at once.

18

"We must go far away from Ulster now," said Deirdre. "I cannot marry Connor."

Deirdre, Naoise and his brothers Áinle and Ardan set off. They traveled all around Ireland but no one would help them because they all feared the anger of King Connor. Finally they sailed to a small island off the coast of Scotland.

There they lived for some time
until one day a messenger
arrived from the king. He
reported that King Connor had
forgiven them.

Deirdre did not trust the message
but the Sons of Uisneach
believed it. Reluctantly, Deirdre
set off with them to Ireland.

On the way she pleaded with
them to turn back but they
would not listen.

When they arrived they were
sent to the house of the Red
Branch Knights, not the king's
castle. Now Deirdre was sure that
a trap had been set for them.

21

Deirdre was right. Soon the house was surrounded. The Sons of Uisneach fought bravely but they were outnumbered. They were seized and brought before Connor. "Who will kill these traitors for me?" asked the king.
None of the Red Branch Knights would kill a fellow knight. Suddenly an unknown warrior from another kingdom stepped forward.
"I will kill them," he shouted. With one blow he cut off the heads of the Sons of Uisneach.

Deirdre screamed and fell dying
to the ground beside the body of
Naoise. So great was her sorrow
that her heart had broken.

Deirdre's father was so angry with
Connor that he left Ulster and
went to live in Connacht. Many
other warriors went with him and
joined the army of Queen Maeve.
This army was later to fight
bloody battles against the Red
Branch Knights.

So Deirdre did bring sorrow and
trouble to Ulster just as the druids
had foretold.

Setanta

Seven year old Setanta was determined to become a member of the famous Red Branch Knights of Ulster. His father, the King of Dundalk, had told him about the special school in Armagh, called the Macra, for the young boys who would one day join the brave warriors.

Setanta pleaded with his parents to let him go there but they refused.

24

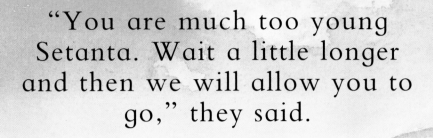

"You are much too young Setanta. Wait a little longer and then we will allow you to go," they said.

Setanta decided he could not wait any longer and so one day he set off for Armagh. It was a long journey but Setanta had his hurley and sliotar to play with. He hit the sliotar far ahead and ran forward to catch it on his hurley stick before it hit the ground.

When Setanta reached the castle of King Connor at Armagh he found the hundred and fifty boys of the Macra gathered on the great plain in front of the castle. Some of them were playing hurling and as this was his favorite game he hurried over to join in. Almost immediately he scored a brilliant goal.

The other boys were furious that this young boy had joined their game uninvited and they attacked him.

Setanta fought bravely. The noise disturbed the king who was playing chess. He sent a servant outside to see what was happening. Setanta was brought before the king.

"I am Setanta, son of the King of Dundalk, your brother. I have come all this way to join the Macra because I want to become one of the Red Branch Knights as soon as I am old enough." The king liked Setanta's brave words and welcomed him to the Macra.

Time passed quickly for
Setanta. He loved his new
life at the Macra.

One day, Culann, the
blacksmith who made spears
and swords for Connor
invited the king, his knights
and Setanta to a feast.

When it was time to set off
for the feast, Setanta was
playing a game of hurling. He
told the king that he would
follow as soon as the game
was finished. The feast began
and Connor forgot to mention
that Setanta would be joining
the party later. Thinking all
his guests had arrived, the
blacksmith unchained his
wolfhound which guarded his
house each night.

As soon as the game was over
Setanta set out. When he
arrived at Culann's house he
heard the deep growls of the
wolfhound. Suddenly the
hound leaped forward out of
the dark to attack. Setanta
saw the sharp teeth bared.
With all his strength Setanta
hurled his sliotar down the
hound's throat. Then he
caught the animal by its hind
legs and dashed it against a
rock. With a loud groan
the wolfhound fell
down, dead.

Inside, the feast party had heard the dog growling. "My nephew Setanta," Connor cried. "I forgot about him." He and the Red Branch Knights rushed out expecting to find the young boy torn to pieces.

Connor was amazed and
delighted to find his nephew
alive and he was proud of his
great strength.

Culann was relieved that the boy was safe but he was sad that he had lost the wolfhound he loved which had faithfully guarded his house every night.

"Let me take the place of your hound until I have trained one of its puppies," said Setanta Culann agreed. From that day on Setanta was called Cú Chulainn which means the Hound of Culainn.

The Salmon of Knowledge

Long ago in Ireland the king had a special army of soldiers called the Fianna to guard him. Cumhall was their most famous leader. His enemies were jealous of him, so they killed him. Cumhall's wife was afraid that her young son Fionn might also be killed.

So she took him to two women
warriors who lived on the slopes
of the Sliabh Bloom Mountains.
She asked the women to teach the
young boy all that a son of
Cumhall should know, for she
knew that one day her son would
become one of the Fianna.

35

At that time, any youth wishing to join the Fianna had to pass very difficult tests. He had to defend himself against the spears of nine men using only a shield; he had to jump over a pole as high as his head; and he had to recite twelve books of poetry.

When the women had taught
Fionn all the fighting skills he
would need, they sent him to
Finnéigeas the poet to learn the
twelve books of poetry.

Finnéigeas lived on the banks of the river Boyne. He had spent many years living beside this river and fishing in it. There was a fish in the Boyne known as the Salmon of Knowledge. The person who caught and ate it would know everything there was to know in the world. Finnéigeas liked the young fair-haired Fionn and agreed to become his teacher.

One day as Fionn was learning
poetry he heard a shout.
He rushed to the river and
there stood Finnéigeas holding
a large salmon.
"Take the fish and cook it for
me please Fionn," he said.
"Remember you must not eat
any of it."

39

Fionn did as he was told. He cleaned the salmon, lit the fire and put the salmon over the fire to cook. All was well until a blister rose on the side of the salmon. Without thinking, Fionn reached out and broke the skin of the blister. In doing so he burned his thumb and sucked it to stop the pain. He finished cooking the fish as Finnéigeas returned.

The old man looked at Fionn
and saw in his eyes the
knowledge he had spent so many
years searching for.
"There is nothing for me to teach
you now," he said sadly. "You
must go to Tara and take your
father's place at the head of the
Fianna. Always use your
knowledge wisely."

Fionn set off at once to join the
Fianna. From then on, whenever
he had a problem, all he had to
do was put his thumb in his
mouth and he had the answer
at once.

Fionn and the Dragon

Fionn said goodbye to Finneigeas and set off. The road to Tara was busy with people arriving for the great festival of Samhain.

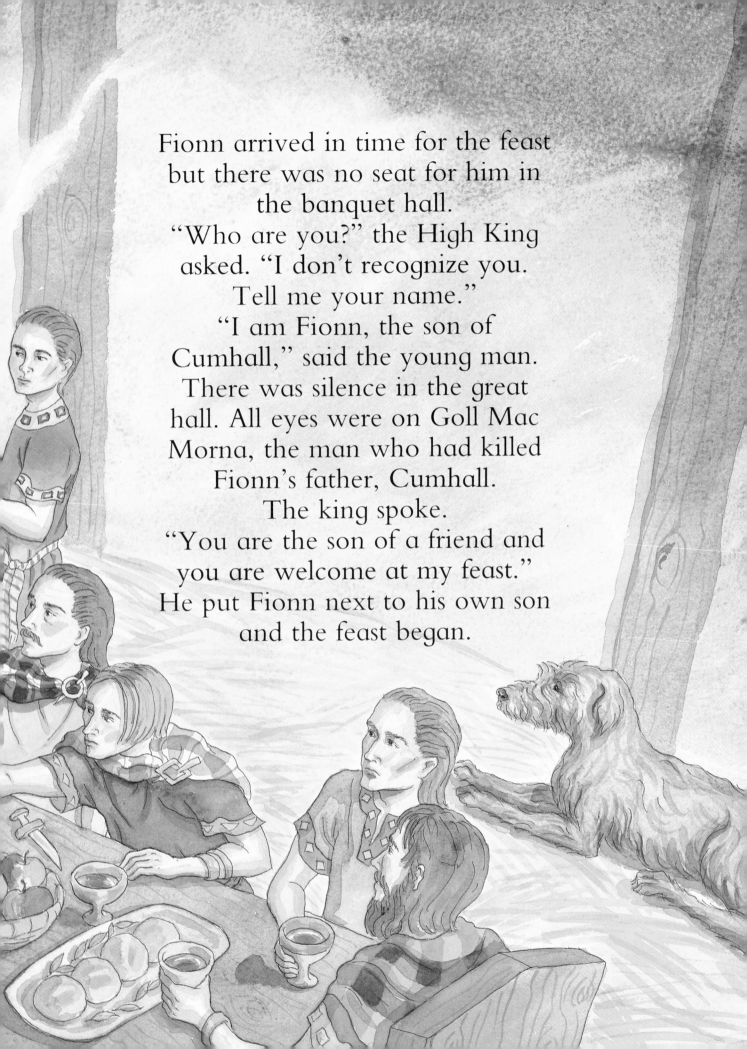

Fionn arrived in time for the feast
but there was no seat for him in
the banquet hall.
"Who are you?" the High King
asked. "I don't recognize you.
Tell me your name."
"I am Fionn, the son of
Cumhall," said the young man.
There was silence in the great
hall. All eyes were on Goll Mac
Morna, the man who had killed
Fionn's father, Cumhall.
The king spoke.
"You are the son of a friend and
you are welcome at my feast."
He put Fionn next to his own son
and the feast began.

During the feast the High
King spoke.
"For the past nine years Tara has
been visited on the festival of
Samhain by an evil spirit. This
spirit appears in the form of a
fire-breathing dragon which
causes great damage.

46

My magicians are powerless.
Many warriors have tried to kill
it but all have failed. Is there
anyone among you who will save
Tara?" the High King asked.
No one spoke. Fionn stood up.
"What reward will be given
to the person who is
successful?" he asked.
"I will grant you whatever you
want," replied the king.
"In that case I will defend Tara
from the evil spirit," said Fionn.

47

Fionn walked to the outer walls
of the city. The sky was dark
and there was no sound to be
heard. The people were
gathered safely inside the walls.
Fionn heard footsteps.

"Who goes there?" he called.
"I am a friend," came the reply.
"I was a friend of your father's
and I have come to repay a
favor your father did for me.
As you know, when the dragon
approaches he plays sweet music.
Anyone who hears this music
falls asleep at once. Take this
magic spear and as soon as the
music begins press it against
your forehead and the music
will have no power over you.
I must hurry away now."
Fionn was left alone.

From the darkness came a low, sweet sound. It was the magic music of the Fairyworld. Immediately Fionn put the spear to his forehead and although the people of Tara fell into a deep sleep Fionn remained awake. The dragon breathed a long blue flame. Fionn aimed and fired the spear. The dragon fell dead on the spot. Fionn cut off its head.

"What is your wish?" the High King asked.
"I ask to be leader of the Fianna as my father was," replied the proud hero.
The High King agreed.

"You have a choice to make," the High King said to Goll Mac Morna. "You can accept Fionn as your leader or you must leave Ireland."

Goll thought for a while and then
spoke to Fionn.
"Here is my hand. I will gladly
serve you."
Once Goll Mac Morna had
submitted the other warriors of
the Fianna followed. So Fionn
became their leader, as his father
before him had been.

Oisín in Tír na n-Óg

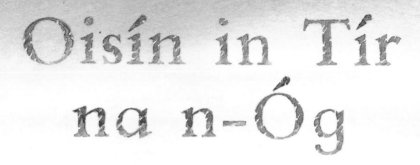

One morning the Fianna were hunting deer on the shores of Loch Léin in Kerry. They saw a beautiful white horse coming towards them. Riding on the horse was the most beautiful woman they had ever seen. She wore a long dress as blue as the summer sky, studded with silver stars, and her long golden hair hung to her waist.

"What is your name and what land have you come from?" asked Fionn, Leader of the Fianna.
"I am Niamh of the golden hair. My father is king of Tír na n-Óg," she replied. "I have heard of a warrior called Oisín. I have heard of his courage and of his poetry. I have come to find him and take him back with me to Tír na n-Óg."

Oisín was the son of Fionn. He
was a great hero and a poet.
"Tell me," Oisín said, "what sort
of a land is Tír na n-Óg?"

"Tír na n-Óg is the land of youth," replied Niamh. "It is a happy place, with no pain or sorrow. Any wish you make comes true and no one grows old there. If you come with me you will find out all this is true."

Oisín mounted the white horse and said goodbye to his father and friends. He promised he would return soon. The horse galloped off over the water, moving as swiftly as a shadow. The Fianna were sad to see their hero go, but Fionn reminded them of Oisín's promise to return soon.

The king and queen of Tír na
n-Óg welcomed Oisín and held
a great feast in his honor. It was
indeed a wonderful land, just as
Niamh had said. He hunted and
feasted and at night he told
stories of Fionn and the Fianna
and of their lives in Ireland.
Oisín had never felt as happy as
he did with Niamh and before
long they were married.

58

Time passed quickly and although he was very happy, Oisín began to think of returning home for a visit. Niamh didn't want him to go, but at last she said "Take my white horse. It will carry you safely to Ireland and back. Whatever happens you must not get off the horse and touch the soil of Ireland. If you do you will never return to me or to Tír na n-Óg."

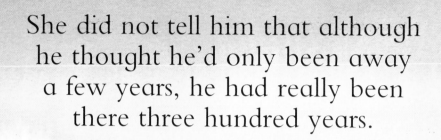

She did not tell him that although
he thought he'd only been away
a few years, he had really been
there three hundred years.

Ireland seemed a strange place to
Oisín when he arrived. There
seemed to be no trace of his
father or the rest of the Fianna.
The people he saw seemed
small and weak to him.

As he passed through Gleann na
Smól he saw some men trying
to move a large stone.
"I will help you," said Oisín. The
men were terrified of this giant on
a white horse. Stooping from his
saddle, Oisín lifted the stone with
one hand and hurled it. With that
the saddle girth broke and Oisín
was flung to the ground.

Immediately the white horse
disappeared and the men saw
before them an old, old man.
They took him to a holy man
who lived nearby.

"Where is my father and the Fianna?" Oisín asked. When he was told that they were long dead he was heartbroken. He spoke of the many deeds of Fionn and the Fianna and their adventures together. He spoke of his time in Tír na n-Óg and his beautiful wife that he would not see again. Although he died soon after, the wonderful stories of Oisín have lived on.

This book has been created and
produced by Zigzag Publishing Ltd,
The Barn, Randolph's Farm, Brighton
Road, Hurstpierpoint, East Sussex
BN6 9EL, England.

Edited by Nicola Wright & Eveleen Coyle
Designed by Ross Thomson
Cover design by Kate Buxton
Production by Zoë Fawcett & Simon Eaton
Color separations by RCS Graphics Ltd, England
Printed by New Interlitho, Italy

This 1995 edition published by Derrydale Books,
distributed by Random House Value Publishing, Inc.
40 Engelhard Avenue
Avenel, New Jersey 07001

Random House
New York • Toronto • London • Sydney • Auckland

ISBN 0-517-14056-X

8 7 6 5 4 3 2 1